A NOTE TO PARENTS

When your children are ready to "step into reading," giving them the right books is as crucial to their development as giving them the right food to eat. **Step into Reading®** books and **Star Wars®** **Jedi Readers** feature exciting stories and information reinforced with lively, colorful illustrations that make learning to read fun, satisfying, and rewarding. We have even taken *extra* steps to keep your child engaged by offering Step into Reading Sticker books, Step into Reading Math books, and Step into Reading Phonics books, in addition to fabulous fiction and nonfiction.

Learning to read, Step by Step:

- **Super Early** books (Preschool–Kindergarten) support pre-reading skills. Parent and child can engage in "see and say" reading using the strong picture cues and the few simple words on each page.
- **Early** books (Preschool–Kindergarten) let emergent readers tackle one or two short sentences of large type per page.
- **Step 1** books (Preschool–Grade 1) have the same easy-to-read type as Early, but with more words per page.
- **Step 2** books (Grades 1–3) offer longer and slightly more difficult text while introducing contractions and clauses. Children are often drawn to our exciting natural science nonfiction titles at this level.
- **Step 3** books (Grades 2–3) present paragraphs, chapters, and fully developed plot lines in fiction and nonfiction.
- **Step 4** books (Grades 2–4) feature thrilling fiction and nonfiction illustrated with exciting photographs for independent as well as reluctant readers.

Remember: The grade levels assigned to the six steps are intended only as guides. Some children ~~ ugh all six steps rapidly; others clim~~ few years. Either way, these bo 'step into reading" for life!

For my Tali and Gabe: "… more than there are stars in the sky—always!" For the "A" Team—many thanks!: Fred Lown, Sandy Wixted, Adine Storer, Gail Harris, David Reider, Helen Forgette, Joseph Tovares, and Chuck Berk. And for my friend and editor, Heidi Kilgras: Always much appreciation and—peace and peaches!

—E.A.

© 2002 Lucasfilm Ltd. & ® or TM where indicated. All rights reserved. Used under authorization. All rights reserved under International and Pan-American Copyright Conventions. Published in the United States by Random House, Inc., New York, and simultaneously in Canada by Random House of Canada Limited, Toronto.

www.randomhouse.com/kids

Official *Star Wars* Web Sites:
www.starwars.com
www.starwarskids.com

Library of Congress Cataloging-in-Publication Data
Arnold, Eric.
Jango Fett : bounty hunter / by Eric Arnold ; illustrated by Valerie Reckert.
p. cm. — (Step into reading. Step 3 book. Star wars Jedi readers)
SUMMARY: Boba Fett's father, Jango, accepts a dangerous mission as a bounty hunter.
ISBN 0-375-81464-7 (trade) — ISBN 0-375-91464-1 (lib. bdg.)
[1. Science fiction.] I. Reckert, Valerie, ill. II. Title. III. Series.
PZ7.A73525 Jan 2002 [Fic]—dc21 2001048841

Printed in the United States of America   April 2002   10 9 8 7 6 5 4 3 2 1

STEP INTO READING, RANDOM HOUSE, and the Random House colophon are registered trademarks of Random House, Inc.

JEDI READERS

STAR WARS

JANGO FETT: BOUNTY HUNTER

A Step 3 Book

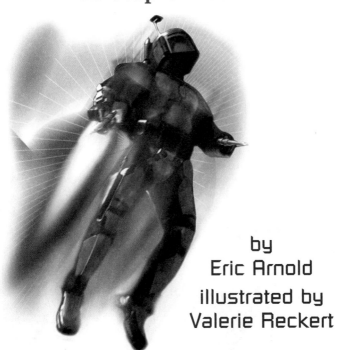

by
Eric Arnold
illustrated by
Valerie Reckert

Random House
New York

1
Father and Son

Slave I dived right for the old energy tower.

"Hold on, Dad!" Boba Fett yelled from inside the cramped cockpit. "This is going to be close!"

"Pull up *now,* Boba!" said Jango Fett.

Boba spiraled the starship upward out of its screeching dive, just missing the tower. *Slave I*'s drive engines roared.

"Go back for the attack," said Jango.

"No problem!" Boba checked the gauges of the weapons systems on board.

"Check your blaster cannon monitor," Jango added.

Boba tightly turned *Slave I* high in the air and zoomed back with the energy tower in his scope.

Boba flipped the switch for the blaster cannons.

"Fire on three ...," Jango commanded. "One, two, *three*!"

Kaboom!

The tower blasted to pieces, raining down into the ocean that covered the planet of Kamino.

"Nice job," said Jango. "You're a fine pilot, Boba, even though you're only ten."

"Well, I take after you, Dad. I am going to be a bounty hunter just like you!" Boba said with a smile.

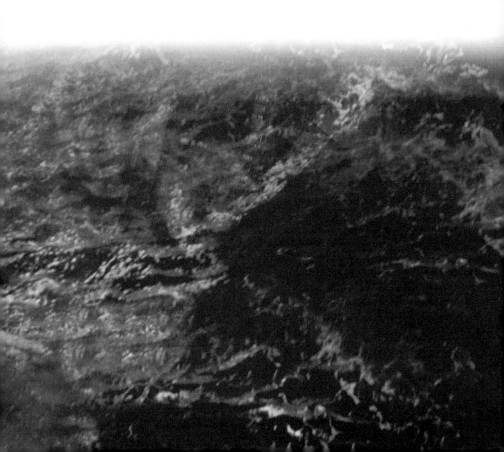

Slave I cruised low over an exercise field. An army of clone troopers marched in formation below.

"It's a dangerous life," Jango said. "See those troopers?"

"Yes."

"They have no control over their destiny. But you and I do. I *chose* to allow the Kaminoans to clone me for their army."

"Yeah, but being a bounty hunter is important. Isn't it?" asked Boba.

"*Listen*, Boba. When there is a job to do, you do it, no matter what. If you choose the life of a bounty hunter, it will not always be clear what side of the law you are on."

"My mind is made up, Dad. I'm ready!" Boba steered *Slave I* toward home.

2
A New Mission

Beeeep! Beeeep!

Jango walked to the communication room in his apartment in Tipoca City. A holoprojector transmission was coming through.

The image of Count Dooku appeared in the air before Jango.

"I am in need of your services again, Jango," said Dooku. "You're the only bounty hunter who can do the job right."

Dooku explained the mission.

"Senator Amidala must be eliminated. With her gone, we will get the Trade Federation's support. This can't wait."

"In that case, I want *double* my usual fee—half up front," Jango demanded.

"Agreed!" Dooku answered sharply. "The job is on Coruscant. I will forward the details to you."

Jango stood at his desk. *This is a big job,* he thought. *I must get started right away. I'll need a partner—someone I can trust.*

Jango scanned through names in his datapad memory bank.

I'll hire Zam Wesell. She's an explosives expert and a changeling. She can take the form of almost any species in the galaxy. Perfect.

Wasting no time, he contacted her on the comm station. "Zam, I have a job for you."

"I'm always game if the price is right, old friend," said Zam.

They arranged to meet at the Outlander Club on Coruscant the next night.

Jango opened the door and spoke with Boba. "I will be gone a few days, son. I have a new mission."

"Take me with you!" Boba begged.

"Not this time," Jango answered. "Taun We will look after you. Keep up with your studies and exercises."

Jango gathered his battle armor and weapons. "You will soon grow into a man, Boba. Your time to go on a mission will come."

As he opened the door to leave, Boba called out, "I'll miss you, Dad."

"I'll miss you, too," Jango said softly.

Boba watched through the window as his father took off in *Slave I* in the driving rains of Kamino.

3
Partners

Jango pushed his way through a crowd of aliens, droids, and humans on a nasty street in Coruscant. He reached the Outlander Club and stepped inside.

Jango scanned the room, looking for Zam. He sat down at a table and waited, ready for anything. He heard a voice behind him say, "Anyone sitting here?"

Jango recognized the voice and turned around. "Right on time, Zam," he said. "Sit down. Let's get to work."

"That's the Jango I know," chuckled Zam. "Never one for small talk! Fill me in."

With his datapad, Jango showed Zam a diagram of the landing platform where the Senator's ship would be landing the next morning. He warned her that the ship would not arrive alone. It would be escorted by three Naboo fighters. Her mission was to plant a thermal detonator that would explode once the Senator's ship touched down.

The plan was all set. Jango and Zam closed the deal with a handshake and got up to leave.

"Leaving so soon?" asked Elan Sleazebaggano, an underworld lowlife. He blocked Zam's way. "Wanna buy some Rancor nail blades?"

Jango pushed him aside.

"Not today, friend," growled Jango.
Elan Sleazebaggano stumbled backward
into a table of droids.

"Let's get out of here," said Jango. He
and Zam walked out of the club.

4
The Decoy

The Naboo cruiser flew along the skylane to the landing platform on Coruscant.

Zam watched from a distance through her electrobinoculars. The Naboo cruiser lowered its boarding ramp.

The Senator and her guards began to exit the craft when suddenly there was a blinding flash and—*kaboooom!* People were hurled to the ground by an explosion. Fragments of the ship flew everywhere!

Zam could see one of the pilots kneeling beside the gravely hurt Senator Amidala. As the pilot removed her helmet, the smoke became too thick for Zam to see anything more.

"Mission accomplished!" Zam gloated.

Meanwhile, Jango waited in *Slave I* for word from Zam. *Beeep! Beeep!*

That must be her on the comlink, thought Jango. But it wasn't Zam.

"The mission failed!" growled an angry Count Dooku. "My sources tell me that Amidala's *decoy* was killed—*not* the Senator!"

Jango kept his cool. "Not a problem. I will go to my next plan."

Jango quickly transmitted the news to Zam via his helmet comlink. *This time, we will have to get closer to strike,* thought Jango.

5
The New Plan

Jango stood waiting on the ledge of a skyscraper.

Vrooooom! A speeder roared up. Zam stepped from her craft.

"My client is getting impatient," said Jango. "We must try a different approach. There can be no mistakes."

He handed her a clear tube. It held two kouhuns—fat centipede-like creatures with deadly stingers. They killed by injecting poison into their victims.

"Take these. Be careful. They're lethal."

Zam took the vial of kouhuns. She put the kouhuns in an ASN-121 droid and guided it by remote to the Senate building, where Amidala was staying. The kouhuns would be unleashed on her while she slept.

"Nothing will go wrong," Zam said.

"I know," Jango responded, then turned to leave.

6
Jedi Alert

Zam watched with a mini–remote monitor as the droid attached itself to the Senator's bedroom window.

The droid shut down the alarm system and cut a small hole in the glass. The kouhuns crawled from the tube through the hole in the window, toward the sleeping Senator.

Suddenly, two Jedi dashed into the room.

Hssss! The kouhuns stood on their hind legs, ready to strike the Senator as she woke up.

"Don't move!" the younger Jedi, a Padawan, screamed. He swiftly whacked the kouhuns in half with his lightsaber.

Zam's screen crackled and went blank!
The Jedi Knight had spotted the droid
outside the window and raced for it. *Crash!*
Diving through the window, he grabbed
the droid as it began to take flight.

The droid is heading this way, Zam thought, *with a Jedi Knight hanging from it!* She contacted Jango via comlink: "The mission has failed. The Jedi are involved."

This is dangerous, Jango thought as he watched from a few blocks away. Security vehicles began swarming the area. *Any chance for me to get to the Senator is ruined.* He started up his jetpack and took off after Zam.

7
The Chase

Zam fired at the droid as it neared her building. She scored a direct hit, and the Jedi Knight tumbled through the sky. *Good!* thought Zam. But a few seconds later, he was scooped up by a racing speeder. The younger Jedi had come to his rescue. Zam hopped into her own speeder and raced away.

Soon the speeders were neck and neck.
Zam took a sharp right turn into a tram
tunnel. The Jedi followed, but they didn't
know a transport was coming from the
other direction, straight at them!

The two speeders braked, turned
around, and raced out just in time! Zam
tried to cut the Jedi off, but their speeder
escaped through a gap between two
buildings. The young Jedi was a crack
pilot!

Zam thought she had lost the Jedi when…*wham!* Something landed on the roof of her speeder. The Padawan had jumped from five stories up! He used the Force to try to get Zam's blaster. As they struggled over the weapon, it went off, blowing a hole in the floor. The speeder went into a nosedive.

Barely gaining control, Zam landed in a sea of sparks—*screech!* The young Jedi flipped head over heels onto the sidewalk.

Zam jumped from the crashed speeder and ran. The Jedi Knight had also landed, and both Jedi tried to catch up with Zam. But she blended in with the crowd and slipped into the Outlander Club.

Jango touched down on a nearby rooftop. He had followed the chase from a safe distance, so he wouldn't be seen. What he saw next surprised him. The Jedi were carrying Zam out of the club's back entrance and into an alley. She was badly wounded!

Jango could not hear the conversation between the Jedi and Zam, but he could read their lips. He feared that Zam would break the bounty hunter code: *Never tell anyone who hired you for a job.*

Jango readied a toxic dart he kept in his utility belt for emergencies. He did not want to use it....

"Who hired you?" the Jedi Knight asked as he lowered Zam to the ground.

Zam glared at the Jedi. "It was a bounty hunter called—"

Jango had no choice but to use the toxic dart now.

Fzzzzt!

The dart struck Zam in the neck. As she died, her body changed into its natural Clawdite form.

Whoosh! Jango quickly jetted off from the rooftop, but not before the Jedi looked up and saw him fly away.

8
A New Hunter

"Okay, Boba, let's try a blind landing one more time," Jango instructed.

"Dad, I've been flying *Slave I* since I was little!"

"Because it flies 'standing up' and lands with its engines down, it takes skill that even a fine pilot must work on, Boba."

"Tell me something I don't know, Dad."

"How about this—my last mission failed." Boba got very quiet as Jango looked at him with dark eyes.

"The Jedi got involved. That's something a bounty hunter doesn't want to happen. But it's the risk you take."

"What do you mean?" asked Boba.

"Powerful people will sometimes come after you. They'll try to stop you from doing what you were hired to do."

"What are you going to do now?" Boba asked.

"I will have to finish this business with the Jedi. It changes everything to have them involved," Jango said thoughtfully.

"I want to help so I can be just like you when I grow up," said Boba.

"Don't worry, I have a feeling you will be, son."